The Boy Who

by Benjamin James Watson

iLLUSTRaTeD by

Went Ape

Richard Jesse Watson

THE BLUE SKY PRESS
An Imprint of Scholastic Inc.
New York

The paper used by Richard Jesse Watson for the paintings in this book was made from elephant dung by Maximus, a papermaking company in Sri Lanka. This grassroots business benefits the environment and the local economy, and it helps save the lives of Asian elephants who damage the crops of farmers. It is sold in various zoos and fair trade stores across the United States and Canada under the company name "Mr. Ellie Pooh." The paintings were made with Sumi ink and acrylic on elephant dung paper.

THE BLUE SKY PRESS

Text copyright © 2008 by Benjamin James Watson

Illustrations copyright © 2008 by Richard Jesse Watson

Library of Congress catalog card number: 2007009704.

ISBN-10: 0-590-47966-0 / ISBN-13: 978-0-590-47966-0

10 9 8 7 6 5 4 3 2 1   08 09 10 11 12

Printed in Singapore   46

First printing, September 2008

For The creator of all Those glorious skipping rocks.
And Thanks, Dad, for The cool pictures—
not bad for a knuckle-walker.
—B.J.W.

For Ben: Ever since we brought you home from
The zoo, you have been like a son To us.
Thank you, Jeston, The perfect jungle boy,
and Beth, The best librarian
a chimp could ever have.
—R.J.W.

Nobody in the history of Alcatraz Elementary School had ever gotten in as much trouble as Benjamin. All day long, his teacher said, **"STOP THAT, BENJAMIN!"**

BuT The MOST TrouBLe he ever goT in was
The day his cLASS weNT on a fieLd Trip
around TowN.

The first stop was The Zoo. Ms. Thunderbum told her class, and especially Benjamin, "Don't Touch The animal cages!"

But, as usual, Benjamin wasn't listening.

"CLass, iT's Time To go back on The bus,"
Ms. Thunderbum caLLed.
"You, Too, Benjamin," she said
To The chimpanzee.

Meanwhile, back in The ape cage, Benjamin was learning how chimpanzees play Tag. "Whoopee!"

The Second Stop on The field Trip was The Library.

MS. Thunderbum announced, "Now, class—and especially Benjamin—we all need To use our quiet Voices."

The Librarian, Miss Hush, read a book aloud to the class.

Once there was a magic rabbit.

The chimp wearing Benjamin's hat saw his reflection in a mirror.

He Thought iT WaS another chimpanzee!

ThaT ape in The mirror copied every SiLLy face he made. He began yeLLing, and The ape in The mirror yeLLed righT back.

"Ooh ooh ahh ahh AHH AHHH AHHHHHHHHHH!"

"STOP THAT, BENJAMIN!" Ms. Thunderbum hissed. "Stop that right now!"

Meanwhile, back at the zoo,
The chimps were checking Benjamin for bugs.

The next stop on the field trip was the grocery store.

HE STARTED A FOOD FIGHT!

"STOP THAT, BENJAMIN! STOP THAT right now!" MS. Thunderbum belLowed. "YOU are acTing Like an animaL!"

Meanwhile, back at the zoo,
Benjamin was making friends.

The LAST STOP on The field Trip was The bank.

Ms. Thunderbum glared at the chimp she called Benjamin.
"Class, we must ALL be on our BEST behavior here!"
That ape would have been good . . .

Just then, as the chimp was swinging on the chandelier . . . a bank robber stormed in!

"STICK 'EM UP!" he snarled,
standing right below the dangling ape.

"Oh, Thank you, Benjamin! You saved us all! You're a hero!" MS. Thunderbum exclaimed until . . .

"YOU'RE NOT BENJAMIN!" shouTed The class. Ms. Thunderbum Shrieked and ran ouT The door.

Back at the zoo, the zookeeper was puzzled. In the distance, he heard Ms. Thunderbum. And what did she yell?

"STOP THAT, BENJAMIN! STOP THAT RIGHT NOW!"

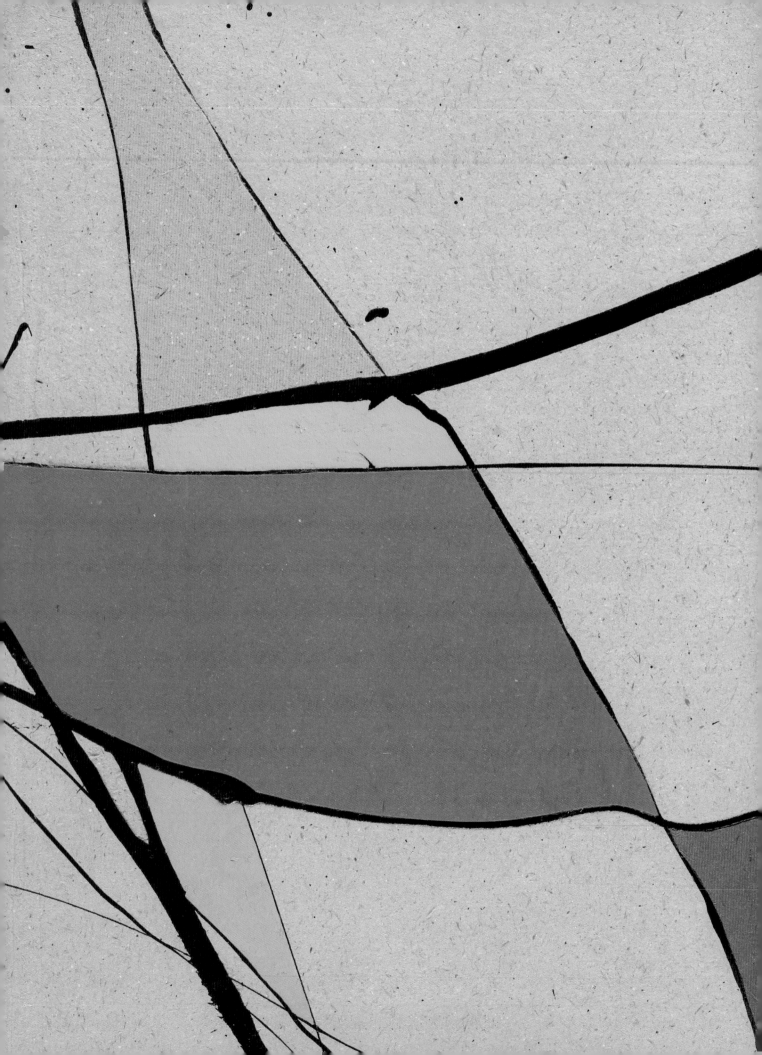